Island in the Sun

WORDS AND MUSIC BY
Harry Belafonte and Irving Burgie

This is my ... ... ple have toiled since time be-gun._

Tho I may sail on ... a sea, Her shores will al - ways be home to me._

Oh, is - land ... the sun, Willed to me_ by my fa - ther's hand,_

All my days_ I will sing in praise Of your for - ests, wa - ters, your shin-ing sand._

To my mother. And thanks to Caro Ness.
A. A.

First published in the United States by Dial Books for Young Readers
A division of Penguin Putnam Inc.
345 Hudson Street • New York, New York 10014

Published in Great Britain by A & C Black (Publishers) Ltd
35 Bedford Row, London WC1R 4JH
"Island in the Sun" Words and Music by Harry Belafonte and Irving Burgie
Copyright © 1956; renewed 1984 by Clara Music Publishing Corporation
(ASCAP)/Cherry Lane Music Publishing Company, Inc. (ASCAP)/Lord Burgess
Music Publishing Company (ASCAP)/DreamWorks Songs (ASCAP).
Worldwide rights for Clara Music Publishing Corporation administered by
Next Decade Entertainment, Inc. (ASCAP)/Worldwide rights for
Lord Burgess Music Publishing Company and DreamWorks Songs
administered by Cherry Lane Music Publishing Company, Inc.
All rights reserved. Used by permission.
Pictures copyright © 1999 by Alex Ayliffe
All rights reserved \ Designed by Pamela Darcy
Printed in Belgium
First Edition
1 3 5 7 9 10 8 6 4 2

Library of Congress Cataloging in Publication Data
Belafonte, Harry, date.
Island in the sun/Harry Belafonte and Lord Burgess;
pictures by Alex Ayliffe.—1st ed.
p.   cm.
Summary: Illustrations accompany the words to a song made popular
by Harry Belafonte, paying tribute to his island childhood.
ISBN 0-8037-2387-3 (trade)
1. Children's songs—Texts. [1. Islands—Songs and music. 2. Songs.] I. Burgie, Irving.
II. Ayliffe, Alex, ill. III. Title. PZ8.3.B3957Is   1999
782.42164'0268—dc21   [E]   98-36175   CIP   AC

The artwork was produced as collage.

Island in the Sun

Harry Belafonte and Lord Burgess

pictures by Alex Ayliffe

Dial Books for Young Readers | New York

This is my island in the sun
Where my people have toiled
since time begun.

Tho I may sail on many a sea,
Her shores will always be home to me.

Oh, island in the sun,
Willed to me by
my father's hand,
All my days
I will sing in praise
Of your forests, waters,
your shining sand.

When morning breaks the heaven on high,
I lift my heavy load to the sky.

Sun comes down with a burning glow,
Mingles my sweat with the earth below.

Oh, island in the sun,
Willed to me by
my father's hand,
All my days
I will sing in praise
Of your forests, waters,
your shining sand.

I see woman on bended knee,
Cutting cane for her family.

I see man at the water's side,
Casting nets at the surging tide.

Oh, island in the sun,
Willed to me by
my father's hand,
All my days
I will sing in praise
Of your forests, waters,
your shining sand.

I hope the day will never come
That I can't awake to the sound of drum.

Never let me miss carnival,
With calypso songs
philosophical.

Oh, island in the sun,
Willed to me by
my father's hand,
All my days
I will sing in praise
Of your forests, waters,
your shining sand.

Island in the Sun

Words and Music by Harry Belafonte and Irving Burgie

This is my island in the sun
Where my people have toiled since time begun.
Tho I may sail on many a sea,
Her shores will always be home to me.

Oh, island in the sun,
Willed to me by my father's hand,
All my days I will sing in praise
Of your forests, waters, your shining sand.

When morning breaks the heaven on high,
I lift my heavy load to the sky.
Sun comes down with a burning glow,
Mingles my sweat with the earth below.

I see woman on bended knee,
Cutting cane for her family.
I see man at the water's side,
Casting nets at the surging tide.

I hope the day will never come
That I can't awake to the sound of drum.
Never let me miss carnival,
With calypso songs philosophical.